DRAGONS EVERYWHERE

Nick Toczek works as a poet, storyteller,
journalist, political researcher, novelist and
stand-up comedian. He has made almost 20,000
public appearances over the past 30 years and
most recently has toured his *Dragons!* show which
includes a real Chinese parading dragon and
a smoke machine.

Sally Townsend trained at Bournemouth,
and works as a freelance illustrator and mural
artist in Surrey. Varied work includes greetings
cards, packaging, books and large frescoes
and murals.

First published 1997 by
Macmillan Children's Books
a division of Macmillan Publishers Ltd
25 Eccleston Place, London SW1W 9NF
and Basingstoke

Associated companies throughout the world

ISBN 0 330 36792 7

1 3 5 7 9 8 6 4 2

A CIP catalogue record for this book is available from the British Library.

Printed by Mackays of Chatham PLC, Chatham, Kent.

DRAGONS EVERYWHERE

by Nick Toczek

Illustrated by Sally Townsend

**MACMILLAN
CHILDREN'S BOOKS**

Contents

Part 1
DRAGONS

Part 2
SOME OF THEIR RELATIVES

For my parents,

JOHN AND EILEEN TOCZEK

Part 1
DRAGONS

Ten Green Dragons

In the cave dwelt dragons ten.
One fell fighting four horsemen.

In the cave dwelt dragons nine.
One went down the deep, dark mine.

In the cave dwelt dragons eight.
Two forgot to hibernate.

In the cave dwelt dragons six.
One dropped dead from politics.

In the cave dwelt dragons five.
One took a dive in overdrive.

In the cave dwelt dragons four.
One got struck by a meteor.

In the cave dwelt dragons three.
One ran off with a chimpanzee.

In the cave dwelt dragons two.
One went onto the King's menu.

In the cave dwelt dragons one.
Laid ten eggs and then was gone.

The Week of the Dragon

Monday's dragon was just an egg
not unlike a chicken's. Were they pulling my leg?

Tuesday's dragon hatched one inch high
with crumpled wings which wouldn't fly
and a roar little more than a squeaky cry.

Wednesday's dragon was the size of a cat.
Passers-by paused at the sight of that.
When a woman bent down to give it a pat
it hissed and spat at her and lit her hat.

Thursday's dragon grew bigger than a goat
with a shiny, scaly, bright green coat.
It grew too fast. For an antidote
we saw the vet. But all he wrote was a useless note
prescribing stuff to cool its throat.

Friday's dragon filled our whole street,
lamp-posts flattening beneath its feet,
porches scorched by nostril heat.
It'd eaten all of the butcher's meat
and a child who'd tried to offer it a sweet,
and next-door's dog as an after-dinner treat.

Saturday's dragon, having learnt to fly,
hovered overhead and blotted out the sky.
Its beating wings. Its terrifying cry.
We were all convinced we were just about to die,
but luckily for us – my family and I –
none of this happened. Let me tell you why.
It *was* just a chicken's egg. They'd told me a lie!

So Sunday's dragon wasn't there at all
till a strange man, selling eggs, came to call . . .

Dragons Everywhere

Mrs Meacher, our gym teacher,
looks at you like she might eatcha.
Anger alters every feature.
She becomes another creature –
winged avenger, screamer, screecher.

Burning breath, much more than warm.
She blisters pupils in her form.
If she's a human, I'm a unicorn.

Then there's Gordon, traffic warden,
ordinary 'n' dull with boredom.
Till he roared 'n' ripped 'n' clawed 'n'
ran amok, all lightning jawed 'n'
flaming tongued 'n' toothed 'n' clawed 'n'

frightening as a thunderstorm.
But underneath his uniform
if there's a human, I'm a unicorn.

Mrs Ritter, babysitter,
TV watcher, silent knitter.
I know why her clothes don't fit her.
She's another fire-spitter,
beastly, battle-scarred 'n' bitter.

      Her bat-like wings have both been shorn,
      but I know that she's dragon-spawn.
      If she's a human, I'm a unicorn.

Mouseman Mervyn, dressed in ratskin,
brings his traps in, catches vermin,
scratches his reptilian chin
with fingernails grown long and thin.
His bloodshot eyes. His evil grin.

      A twisted figure, worn and torn,
      who can't recall where he was born.
      If he's a human, I'm a unicorn.

Miss McPeake, our glum shopkeeper,
avaricious treasure-heaper,
piles 'em high and sells 'em cheaper.
People-server and floor-sweeper,
deep down, though, she'd be Grim Reaper.

Customers all sense her scorn.
One day they'll meet her with claws drawn.
If she's a human, I'm a unicorn.

The family that live next door
seem quite all right, but nightly roar
and smoke-stains ruin their decor.
And each of them's a carnivore –
I've seen them eating meat that's raw.

A mountain cave on the Matterhorn's
where each first saw the light of dawn.
If they're all human, I'm a unicorn.

And as for me, I'm feeling strange,
all aches and pains and bad migraines.
Soon parts of me'll start to change,
my limbs and body rearrange,
and I'll become quite dangerous,

grow rows of teeth like rose-bush thorns
and skin as tough as rhino horn,
and be a dragon, not a unicorn.

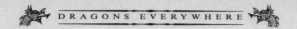
Blubberbelly Wobblewalk Stumblebum Smith

When I was young, I made friends with
Blubberbelly Wobblewalk Stumblebum Smith,
a proper live dragon, not just a myth.

Lonely and large as a monolith,
Blubberbelly Wobblewalk Stumblebum Smith
had no parents, kin or kith.

One day I was cruel. He left forthwith,
Blubberbelly Wobblewalk Stumblebum Smith,
for a secret place he called his frith.

I often wish I'd made up with
Blubberbelly Wobblewalk Stumblebum Smith,
who never returned after our daft tiff.

Was he real or merely a myth?
Blubberbelly Wobblewalk Stumblebum Smith,
the dragon I used to be friends with.

The Day the Dragons Won the Lottery

The day the dragonry won the lottery
they got staggery, swiggery, blotto-ry,
ziggery-zaggery, teetery, tottery,
proudly swaggery,
draggery faggery,
loudly braggery. Rich or what-ery?
When the dragonry won the lottery.

Oops! A snaggery . . . Oh no nottery!
Just a tenner is all they gottery.
What a calamity! Sniffery snottery.
This is most certainly not what it ought to be.
Cursery, slaggery, weepery, watery.
Utterly agony. Heckery! Rottery!
When the dragonry won the lottery.

Song of the Dragon-Slayer

Oh, the only good dragon,
the only good dragon,
the only good dragon's a dead 'un.

From mystic, pre-Christian, weaving and threading
Great Worm that is winter-sky grey, grim and leaden,
through winged English Green and rapacious Welsh
  red 'un,
to deceptively decorous Orient-bred 'un,

the only good dragon,
the only good dragon,
the only good dragon's a dead 'un.

I take drastic action to stop 'em from spreading.
The ground all around is left darkened and bled on.
My blade hacks their necks till each beast has no
  head on,
so saving the souls they would surely have fed on.

The only good dragon,
the only good dragon,
the only good dragon's a dead 'un.

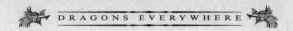

Finding a Dragon that'll Finish our Food

We're children. We're choosy.
We're fussy. We're picky.
Don't want food that's oozy
or slimy or sticky.
Leave heaps and whole slices
from each of those courses
you serve up in spices
or herbs or thick sauces.
Whatever you make us,
just count yourself lucky
if we don't pull faces
or moan that it's yucky.

Yet you say it's rude of us, leaving our food.
But who'll nosh our noodles or feed on our peas?
We need a fine dragon who'll dine on all these:
our spam, spuds and spinach, our strong stinky cheese,
lentils and lettuces, pale tripe and mustard,
large lumpy dumplings and great globs of custard.
You'd best find a beast that you know licks its lips
at kippers and leeks and asparagus tips,
parsnips and turnips and marrows and swedes,
haggises, cabbages, cress and such weeds.
With luck, it'll suit the great big-bellied brute
to pig out on pork pies and purple beetroot.
And bring us a beastie to sit up and beg
for the runniest bits of a breakfast boiled egg.

We're children. We're choosy.
We're fussy. We're picky.
Don't want food that's oozy
or slimy or sticky.

So drag out a dragon that's certain to rid me
of slithery liver and leathery kidney;
which sometimes devours entire cauliflowers;
a dragon quite barmy for brawn or salami,
mad about marrows, mincemeat, minestrone,
prunes, prawns and porridge and cold macaroni.
We need, now, a creature who'd be cock-a-hoop
for oysters and olives and old oxtail soup;

a beast keen on onions and dark aubergines,
broccoli, rhubarb and heaps of broad beans,
cockles and mussels and salady greens,
horseradish sauce and whole tins of sardines.

Whatever you make us,
just count yourself lucky
if we don't pull faces
or moan that it's yucky.

So please help to find us a beast of the kind
who'll finish off platefuls of thick bacon rind;
a great gherkin-gobbler, a greedy and good 'un,
who'll eat up our meatballs and see off black puddin';
a huge hot-breath creature who, quite without worries,
could casually swallow the strongest of curries.
Yes, we've a fine feast for a full-bellied beast
who'll merrily munch on a big bunch of celery.
Why, I bet a dragon's great fire-proof snout
could even consume an entire Brussels sprout.

We're children. We're choosy.
We're fussy. We're picky.
Don't want food that's oozy
or slimy or sticky.

But give us a dragon that's willing to eat
our vilest of veges, our fattiest meat,
our foulest of fruits, our unsavoury sweet,
and mealtimes would magically turn out a treat.

The Dragon in the Cellar

There's a dragon!
There's a dragon!
There's a dragon in the cellar!
Yeah, we've got a cellar-dweller.
There's a dragon in the cellar.

He's a cleanliness fanatic,
takes his trousers and his jacket
to the dragon from the attic
who puts powder by the packet
in a pre-set automatic
with a rattle and a racket
that's disturbing and dramatic.

There's a dragon!
There's a dragon!
There's a dragon in the cellar
with a flame that's red 'n' yeller.
There's the dragon in the cellar . . .

. . . and a dragon on the roof
who's only partly waterproof,
so she's borrowed an umbrella
from the dragon in the cellar.

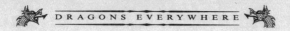

There's a dragon!
There's a dragon!
There's a dragon in the cellar!
If you smell a panatella
it's the dragon in the cellar.

And the dragon from the study's
helping out his cellar buddy,
getting wet and soap-suddy
with the dragon from the loo
there to give a hand too,
while the dragon from the porch
supervises with a torch.
Though the dragon from the landing,
through a slight misunderstanding,
is busy paint-stripping and sanding.

There's a dragon!
There's a dragon!
There's a dragon in the cellar!
Find my dad, and tell the feller
there's a dragon in the cellar . . .

. . . where the dragon from my room
goes zoom, zoom, zoom
in a cloud of polish and spray-perfume,
cos he's the dragon whom
they pay to brighten up the gloom
with a mop and a duster and a broom, broom, broom.

There's a dragon!
There's a dragon!
There's a dragon in the cellar!
Gonna get my mum and tell her
there's a dragon in the cellar.

How the Dragon Became Heroic

That vicious rapscallion
grew colder and harder,

dragged knight from his stallion
with relish and ardour,

slew German, Italian
and Dane for his larder,

drove back a battalion
from here to Granada,

sank each Spanish galleon
that formed The Armada

to earn a medallion
as our nation's guarder.

A Season for Dragons

Between childhood and fairy tales
stretch wonderment and winding trails
through summer days and wooded dales
where leaves grow green as dragon-scales.

But, as we age, the picture pales
of maidens, knights and Holy Grails.
The "I've-no-time-for-that" prevails
to dull the colours and details.

Great shadows fall on hills and vales
as clouds more corpulent than whales
roll overhead on wings like sails
that beat the air like threshing-flails.

And branches thrash like serpents' tails,
and summer somersaults and fails,
while winds are whipped to autumn gales
that howl the way a creature wails.

Hollow as caves from which it hails
comes burning breath this beast exhales.
The tongue of flame that this entails
leaves leaves as brown as rusted nails.

Being a Dragon . . .

Being a dragon is cool as ice.
Being a dragon is nice, nice, nice.
Whatever it costs, it's worth the price
cos being a dragon is nice.

When you're a dragon, it's fine to fly.
Bag the best wings money can buy.
Drop 'em in a vat of sky-green dye
then hang them, bat-like, out to dry.
Shoofly pie. Shoofly pie.
When you're a dragon, it's fine to fly.

Being a dragon is cool as ice.
Being a dragon is nice, nice, nice.
Whatever it costs, it's worth the price
cos being a dragon is nice.

When you're a dragon, you love your claws.
Use hardware stores when you're stealing yours.
Get stainless ones, cos they're good for wars
or settling scores or breaking laws.
Patio doors. Patio doors.
When you're a dragon, you love your claws.

Being a dragon is cool as ice.
Being a dragon is nice, nice, nice.
Whatever it costs, it's worth the price
cos being a dragon is nice.

When you're a dragon, you gargle fire.
Never buy flames. It's better to hire.
Then ignite the tobacco in an old man's briar
and later light his funeral pyre.
Tractor tyre. Tractor tyre.
When you're a dragon, you play with fire.

Being a dragon is cool as ice.
Being a dragon is nice, nice, nice.
Whatever it costs, it's worth the price
cos being a dragon is nice.

The Death of a Scottish Dragon

A young

dragon named Keith
with hundreds of teeth
above and beneath

his tongue

lived north of Leith
till killed on the heath
near cold Cowdenbeath.

They flung

earth onto Keith,
took a sword from its sheath
and on it a wreath

was hung.

Pub-Talk

In the bar of The George and Dragon
they'll serve you a foaming flagon
of English ale
and tell you a tale
of battling beast and of bragging.

Swaggering knights, given a scragging,
in agony, staggering, bloodied and flagging,
fall dead or dying,
cruel fate denying
them victory over the dragon.

Now, drinking is good at ungagging,
and legend sets local tongues wagging . . .
That old dragon's den,
seen by pit-rescue men,
had many a full money bag in.

For hundreds of years it's had swag in
since Georgie, a young scallywag in
a suit of cheap tin
did the dreadful beast in
with no sword, just a bread-knife zigzagging.

In the bar of The George and Dragon
they'll serve you a foaming flagon
of English ale
and spin you that tale
of battling beast and of bragging.

The Beastly Dragon

The dragon, the dragon's a beastly beast,
its face all crumpled up and creased.
It should be jailed and not released.
Instead, it's out there, unpoliced.

The dragon, the dragon's a beastly beast,
a fire-breathing, winged artiste
that's dangerous, to say the least.
It thinks of people as a feast.

The dragon, the dragon's a beastly beast
that has no faith in church or priest,
and though their numbers have decreased,
they're still out west and in the east.

The dragon, the dragon's a beastly beast
that feeds on food that's not deceased
till caked in blood and thoroughly greased,
its temper worse, its size increased.

The dragon, the dragon's a beastly beast
From life that's found in lumps of yeast
to rhino, whale or wildebeest,
the dragon, the dragon's the beast of beasts.

Troglodytic Owner-Occupier

Old flier with a bellyful of fire
that's hotter than a deep-fat frier,
your tongue is tougher than a tyre,
thicker and harder and drier.
You've the appetite of a vampire.

Old flier with a bellyful of fire,
you're driven by desire to acquire.
You trickster, rogue and liar.
You've eyes like snakes', but slyer.
They're sharp as thorns on briar.

Old flier with a bellyful of fire,
mister mayhem-multiplier.
Your cry's a terrifier,
the sound of a suffering choir
entangled in barbed wire.

Old flier with a bellyful of fire,
soaring higher than church and spire.
You're lord and magnifier,
his dragonship, esquire,
arrogant, for all to admire.

Speaking Dragonese

And do you do just as you please?
And are you keen on killing sprees?
And do you speak in Dragonese?

Do you, as everyone agrees,
enjoy these joyless jamborees,
pursuing everyone who flees;
a heartless sword of Damocles
descending on these refugees?
And do you speak in Dragonese?

And of the people whom you seize,
do you chew through each of these
as though they were just chunks of cheese?
And are your legs like trunks of trees,
your hide as hard as manganese?
And do you speak in Dragonese?

Are you immune to most disease,
an unkind kind of Hercules,
a piece of slime, a slice of sleaze
whose mind despises all it sees
through eyes as cold as dungeon keys?
And do you speak in Dragonese?

Does weather warm a few degrees
whenever you so much as sneeze?
And is your breath the devil's breeze,
a howling, haunted, heated wheeze,
a wind to blow till Hell shall freeze?
And do you dream in Dragonese?

The Strength of Dragons

All them dragons, 'ard as nails,
bend steel girders wi' their tails,
Green in England, red in Wales,
'omes in caves and dungeon jails
reek of smoke and old entrails,
'oarding gold and guarding grails,
wing-span wide as galleon sails.

All them dragons, tough as bricks,
'atched from eggs, like nestling chicks,
eyes as cold as old oil-slicks.
Vandalizing lunatics,
they knock 'ole villages for six,
'ead-butt castle walls for kicks
and smash 'em up like matchsticks.

All them dragons, built like boots,
bullet-proof in scaly suits,
are cruel and calculating brutes.
Night-time flights down secret routes
to meet up cos they're in cahoots.
Vile and vicious in disputes,
they share nefarious pursuits.

All them dragons, rough as rocks,
anarchic and unorthodox,
'ave body parts like concrete blocks.
Each 'as a gob-o'-teeth that locks
like thief-proof vault or strongbox.
These beasts gang up in flaming flocks
and armoured knights are laughing stocks.

The Survival of Ivan the Wyvern

Meet Ivan the Wyvern.
This dragon's a live 'un,
the last of his kind still surviving.

Ivan, our Wyvern,
jacks his nine-to-five in,
convinced his good fortune's reviving.

Ivan the Wyvern
loves ducking 'n' diving,
and tells us that soon he'll be thriving.
He has this great plan he's contriving:
'The World of Ivan the Wyvern'.

His cave's now a drive-in
that's got an archive in,
a cafe to eat in, a disco to jive in.

But Ivan the Wyvern
has problems deriving
from half his staff skiving
and rivals conniving
and thereby depriving
his business of funding for fending off bills now arriving.

The last bits of loot he's been hiving
fall short of the thousands he needs to enliven
his fast-fading chance of surviving.
So, pity poor Ivan the Wyvern.

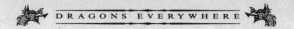

Part 2

SOME OF THEIR RELATIVES

Nature Made the Alligator

Longer, leaner, lighter, straighter,
nature made the alligator.

Underwater navigator,
denizen of the Equator,
bed of reeds or muddy crater.

Longer, leaner, lighter, straighter,
nature made the alligator.

Made its greed grow ever greater,
predatory, patient waiter,
sneaky, silent prey-locator.

Longer, leaner, lighter, straighter,
nature made the alligator.

Cool and crafty calculator,
cruel and creeping infiltrator,
sudden-action operator.

Longer, leaner, lighter, straighter,
nature made the alligator.

Animal de-animator,
river-bank de-populator,
fish-farm thief and devastator.

Longer, leaner, lighter, straighter,
nature made the alligator.

A Happy Appetite

Oh, the crocodile, the crocodile is happy.
And all the while, all the Nile is flappy
cos a mile of highly sharpened teeth, all gappy,
are revealed when the crocodile is happy.

Oh, the crocodile, the crocodile is happy.
Yet we know the wily chappy
's friendly smile is snappy
which is why the silent crocodile is happy.

Oh, the crocodile, the crocodile is happy.
But a silent crocodile is a violent crocodile.
With his vile and toothy trap he
'll slyly satisfy his appy-
tite. Oh-oh . . . !

The crocodile, the crocodile is happy . . .
'SNAP!'

A Loss of Flame and Flight

When dragon got caught in a blizzard
the weather extinguished his gizzard.
So bitten by frost
that his wings were lost,
he lived on . . . as merely a lizard.

Dining Out With Danger!

When you date an alligator,
tell the chef and warn the waiter
there and then. It's too late later.
Dwell on it, advise them well.

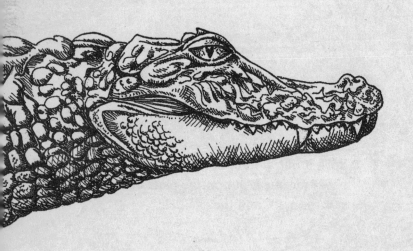

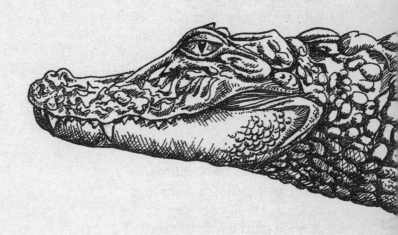

Say your mate's an alligator.
Spell it out: potato-hater;
needs raw meat put on the plate or
eats the staff, and the clientele.

The Visitin' Griffin

We once had a griffin
turn up to take tiffin
back at the old place.

A griffin for tiffin!
We all thought: "How spiffin'!",
me and the staff and His Grace.

But I saw His Grace stiffen
and the butler start sniffin',
Each gave a grim grimace.

A maid murmured: "It's niffin'!",
another: "It's whiffin'!",
a third simply said: "That ain't nayce!"

Thus angered, the griffin
gave butler a biffin';
and, after a bit of a chase,

gave cook quite a duffin',
said: "I ain't done nuffin',"
while she wiped the blood off her chiffon and lace.

Then, calmly, the griffin
picked up a fresh muffin

and carried on stuffin' its face . . .
But His Grace had that griffin
drummed right out and driven,
forbidden from gracin' the place.

It's years since I've seen a griffin.
I suppose, there are still a few livin';
but at least, now, they're not commonplace.

Some Salamanders

Some salamanders say your name.
Some salamanders pray for fame.
Some salamanders slay and maim.

Some salamanders may show shame.
Some salamanders, they take aim.
Some salamanders sway when lame.

Some salamanders lay the blame.
Some salamanders pay that claim.
Some salamanders weigh the same.

Some salamanders play the game.
Some salamanders stay quite tame.
Some salamanders wade through flame.

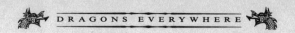

Where the Salamander Sat

Oh, a salamander sat in an inferno
writing letters to his mother to let her know
that he'd met a lovely lizard in Salerno.
The salamander sat
the salamander sat
the salamander sat in an inferno.

Oh, the salamander sat in an inferno.
He was scribbling away while sipping Pernod
though I'll never know quite why he didn't burn. Oh,
the salamander sat
the salamander sat
the salamander sat in an inferno.

Also published by Macmillan

DRAGONS
Fire-Breathing Poems
by Nick Toczek

The Dragon Who Ate
Our School

The day the dragon came to call
she ate the gate, the playground wall
and, slate by slate, the roof and all,
the staffroom, gym, and entrance hall.

And every classroom, big or small.

So . . .
She's undeniably great.
She's absolutely cool,
the dragon who ate
the dragon who ate
the dragon who ate our school.

A selected list of poetry books available from Macmillan

The prices shown below are correct at the time of going to press. However, Macmillan Publishers reserve the right to show new retail prices on covers which may differ from those previously advertised.

DRAGONS
Fire-breathing poems, by Nick Toczek   £3.50

DRAGONS EVERYWHERE
More fire-breathing poems, by Nick Toczek   £3.50

DRACULA'S AUNTIE RUTHLESS
And other petrifying poems, chosen by David Orme   £2.99

NOTHING TASTES QUITE LIKE A GERBIL
And other vile verses, chosen by David Orme   £2.99

THE SECRET LIVES OF TEACHERS
Revealing rhymes, chosen by Brian Moses   £3.50

'ERE WE GO!
Football poems, chosen by David Orme   £2.99

YOU'LL NEVER WALK ALONE
More football poems, chosen by David Orme   £2.99

All Macmillan titles can be ordered at your local bookshop or are available by post from:

Book Service by Post
PO Box 29, Douglas, Isle of Man IM99 1BQ

Credit cards accepted. For details:
Telephone: 01624 675137
Fax: 01624 670923
E-mail: bookshop@enterprise.net

Free postage and packing in the UK.
Overseas customers: add £1 per book (paperback)
and £3 per book (hardback).